D0777933

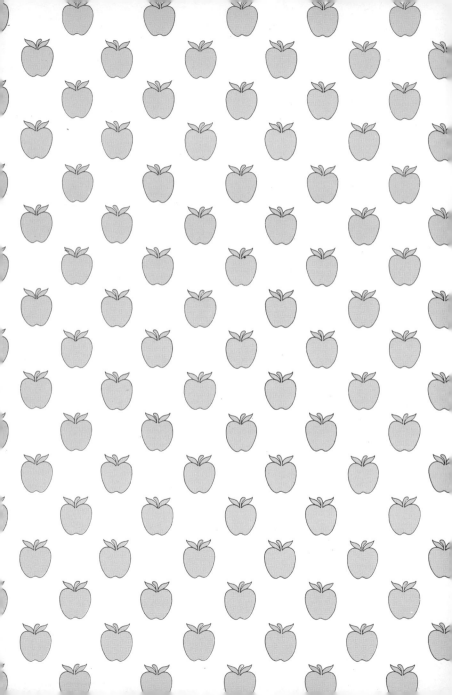

Originally published under the title *Dagobert-Dragon à l'école*
by Gautier-Languereau, Paris
Translation from the French by Didi Charney
© Gautier-Languereau, 1987
Aladdin Books
Macmillan Publishing Company
866 Third Avenue, New York, NY 10022
Collier Macmillan Canada, Inc.
First Aladdin Books edition 1988
Printed in Italy
ISBN 0-689-71192-1

10 9 8 7 6 5 4 3 2 1

The Day the Dragon Came to School

by Marie Tenaille

illustrated by
Violayne Hulné

Aladdin Books
Macmillan Publishing Company
New York

Daniel the dragon flew into town and crept into the second-grade classroom. He'd come to see what school was like.

From the start, he felt he didn't belong. "Oh, no," he said to himself. "I can't stay here. I'm too big, too green, and I don't look like any of the other kids. I won't fit in."

Too late. He'd already been discovered. The students had heard his terrified snorts.

"Hey, look," they said. "Look at the new student."

But just then they had to turn their attention to Miss Stern, who was writing vocabulary words on the blackboard.

The more nervous Daniel became, the louder he snorted! No one could concentrate on anything else.

Cindy whispered, "Wow! A real dragon. He's beautiful. Did you come to class for the spelling lesson?" she asked the dragon.

"Snort," said Daniel, who was terribly embarrassed.

"What's your name?" the students asked.

"It's Daniel Dragon," he said. "Or Danny, to my friends."

"Please breathe a little fire for us."

Daniel opened his mouth…and flames burst out. Miss Stern jumped and said, "Daniel, we don't play with fire in the classroom. Spell the word *flame* for me."

"But they don't teach spelling where he comes from," cried the students, afraid he wouldn't be able to spell it.

"Okay, Daniel," said Miss Stern. "Show us what you *do* know."

Daniel the dragon drew himself up and beat his beautiful scaly tail against the desks. What a wonderful sound it made!

"Hooray!" cried the delighted students.
"Why don't you sing us a song instead,"
suggested Miss Stern.

"Sing 'Old MacDonald,'" Cindy called out.

"We're making him nervous," said Larry.
"Be brave, Daniel. We'll help you get started....
You're such a beautiful dragon."

Everyone could hear his scales clanking together. Finally, Daniel stood up, scared but determined. His new classmates urged him on. Plucking up courage, he began:

Old MacDonald had a farm
EE YI EE YI O.
And on his farm he had a dragon
EE YI EE YI O.

The students applauded.

"Very good, Daniel," said Miss Stern, "and now it's time to get back to our spelling lesson."

Daniel put his head down on a desk and burst into tears. Even the teacher was afraid she'd spoken too harshly to him.

"He's crying dragon tears," said Lucy. "I'm going to try to cheer him up if I can."

"How can we?" asked Arthur. "When he's angry or unhappy, his scales get too hot to touch."

"He'll get used to us," said the teacher. "Now, back to the spelling lesson. Please pay attention!"

Miss Stern turned around to write on the blackboard, but a tremendous grumble from Daniel made her jump.

"He's bored!" He's yawning!" cried Cindy. "I saw all his teeth and his tongue—it's pale pink!"

"Oh, well, it's time for gym," sighed Miss Stern. "Come on, Daniel. Follow the others!"

"Okay, let's go, everyone. Three times around the schoolyard," called the gym instructor, Mr. Cross.

"Danny is already so hot," said Lucy. "Does he have to run, too?"

"Yes, just like everyone else," said Mr. Cross.
"What for?" panted Daniel. "I can fly."

"Mr. Cross," cried the other students, "his scales are burning up. He's got to stop. This isn't good for him!"

"Let's move on to long jumping now," said the gym teacher.

When Daniel heard that, he smiled to himself, ran to the head of the line, and jumped...what a terrific jump!

"Thirty feet," beamed Mr. Cross. "Who's next?"

Daniel puffed himself out with pride, only a little embarrassed for having cheated by using his wings.

"Hooray, Daniel," his classmates whispered, so Mr. Cross wouldn't hear. "You used your wings! If only we were dragons, we could do that, too!"

Gym was over and it was time for lunch. Everyone in Miss Stern's class wanted to sit with Daniel.

"Don't push. There's room for everyone," said Mrs. Cook.

"Snort!" said Daniel, totally comfortable now. And with one gulp, he swallowed a whole plate of sausages and mashed potatoes. Then he asked for more. Brian, who was hungry, started to cry.

"Don't cry, Brian," said Lucy. "It's not his fault. He just has a dragon's appetite." Then she gave the dragon her lunch, too. Larry gave him some cheese and Cindy donated her chocolate pudding. Everyone gave him something tasty to eat.

But even a dragon's stomach has its limits! Suddenly, Daniel went white and put his paws on his stomach. What a stomachache he had!

So, instead of returning to class, he went to the nurse, accompanied by Cindy, Lucy, Larry, and Arthur.

"Come and get him for recess," said Miss Sweet, the nurse. "He'll be fine, once he's lain down for a bit and drunk some mint tea."

Later that afternoon, Daniel felt well enough to play. He was very popular in the schoolyard. His scales sparkled in the sun.

To delight the children, he flapped his wings. Daniel even gave out autographs! And he allowed the bravest ones to touch his crest. It got very hot when he was happy.

"Will he be staying for the spelling bee?"
the students asked Miss Stern.

"No, he won't," she replied. "Daniel misses
his parents and must go home. And I'm sure
he can't wait to tell everyone there about his
day in second grade!"

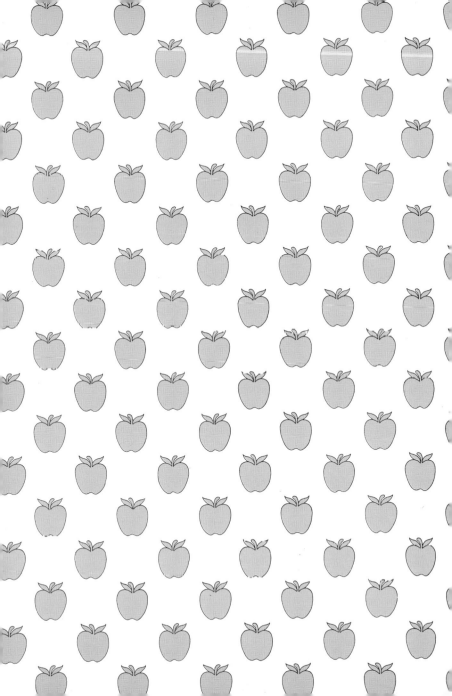